Katie Woo

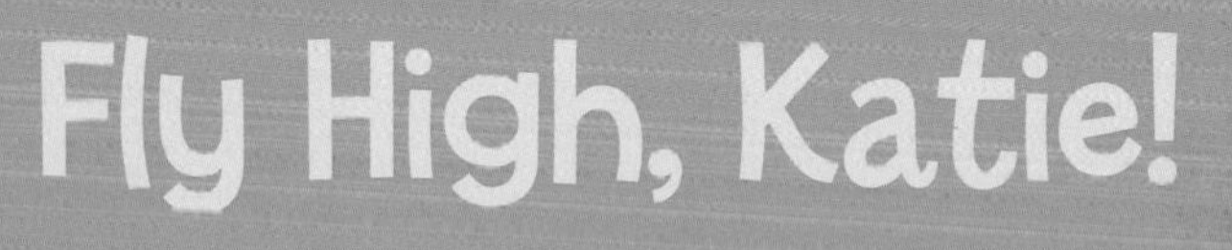

by Fran Manushkin

illustrated by Tammie Lyon

PICTURE WINDOW BOOKS
a capstone imprint

Katie Woo is published by Picture Window Books
a Capstone Imprint
1710 Roe Crest Drive
North Mankato, Minnesota 56003
www.capstonepub.com

Library of Congress Cataloging-in-Publication Data
Manushkin, Fran, author.
Fly high, Katie / by Fran Manushkin; illustrated by Tammie Lyon.
pages cm. — (Katie Woo)
Summary: Katie is flying to Florida to visit her grandmother, but she has never been on an airplane before.
ISBN 978-1-4795-2175-3 (library binding)
ISBN 978-1-4795-2354-2 (paperback)
1. Airplanes—Juvenile fiction. 2. Air travel—Juvenile fiction. 3. Chinese Americans—Juvenile fiction. [1. Airplanes—Fiction. 2. Air travel—Fiction. 3. Chinese Americans—Fiction.] I. Lyon, Tammie, illustrator. II. Title. III. Series: Manushkin, Fran. Katie Woo.

PZ7.M3195Fl 2014
[E]—dc23 2013028513

Art Director: Kay Fraser
Graphic Designer: Kristi Carlson

Photo Credits:
Greg Holch, pg. 26
Tammie Lyon, pg. 26

Printed in the United States of America.
032017 010362R

Table of Contents

Chapter 1

Flying Is Fun

Pedro was showing Katie his model airplane.

"I'm going to Florida," said Katie. "Soon I'll be flying, too."

“No way,” teased Pedro.

“Your arms will get tired.”

“You are silly!” said Katie.

“I’m flying in an airplane.

It’s my first time.”

“Flying is fun,” said JoJo.

“You’ll love it.”

Katie and her mom and dad hurried to the airport. They each had a suitcase. Katie also had her teddy bear.

They rushed to the counter to check their suitcases, then waited in a long line to get on the plane.

"When will this be fun?" Katie wondered.

Chapter 2

Takeoff

Finally, they got on the plane. As Katie buckled her seat belt, she said, "I wonder if my teddy bear needs a seat belt too?"

Katie reached for her bear, but he wasn't there!

"Where's Teddy?" she asked.

"I don't know," said her mom. "He was with us when we checked in."

“We have to run back and get him!” cried Katie.

“We can’t,” said her dad. “The plane is about to take off.”

Zoom! The plane sped down the runway. Then it flew up, up, UP!

Everything on the ground got smaller and smaller.

"Poor Teddy," said Katie. "You are all alone down there."

Katie watched the clouds floating by. One looked like a tiger, and one looked just like Teddy.

Katie's mom gave her some orange juice. Whoops! The plane hit a bump, and the juice spilled on her lap.

"Yikes!" yelled Katie. "What a mess!"

"JoJo told me that flying is fun," groaned Katie. "Maybe it is for birds, but not for me. And I miss my Teddy so much."

"Folks," said the captain, "buckle your seat belts. We will be flying through some turbulence."

"What's that?" asked Katie.

"That's when air gets bumpy," said Katie's mom.

The plane began rocking up and down.

"Wow!" Katie smiled. "This is like riding a pony. It's fun!"

"Soon you'll be seeing Grandma," said Katie's dad. "That will be fun too."

"For sure!" agreed Katie.

Chapter 3

Big Landing

After a while, the ride was smooth again. Katie saw trees and a pretty river shining in the sun. She drew a picture to show Pedro and JoJo.

"We are almost there," said Katie's mom.

The plane flew lower and lower — and *whoosh* — they were back on the ground!

"Where is my suitcase?"

Katie wondered.

"You'll see," said her dad.

"Follow me."

"The suitcases will be coming out here," said Katie's dad. "It's called a carousel because it goes round and round."

Katie watched for her bag. She waited . . . and waited.

And what did she see? Teddy!

He looked happy to see her too.

"So that's where he went," said Katie's dad. "He was checked in with our suitcases."

"And here's Grandma," shouted Katie.

She hugged Teddy and Grandma tight.

"This vacation will be great," said Katie.

It already was.

About the Author

Fran Manushkin is the author of many popular picture books, including *Baby, Come Out!*; *Latkes and Applesauce: A Hanukkah Story*; *The Tushy Book*; *The Belly Book*; and *Big Girl Panties*. There is a real Katie Woo — she's Fran's great-niece — but she never gets in half the trouble of the Katie Woo in the books. Fran writes on her beloved Mac computer in New York City, without the help of her two naughty cats, Chaim and Goldy.

About the Illustrator

Tammie Lyon began her love for drawing at a young age while sitting at the kitchen table with her dad. She continued her love of art and eventually attended the Columbus College of Art and Design, where she earned a bachelor's degree in fine art. After a brief career as a professional ballet dancer, she decided to devote herself full time to illustration. Today she lives with her husband, Lee, in Cincinnati, Ohio. Her dogs, Gus and Dudley, keep her company as she works in her studio.

Glossary

buckle (BUHK-uhl)—to fasten a seat belt

carousel (CARE-uh-sel)—a revolving platform

groan (GROHN)—to make a long, low sound because you are suffering or unhappy

model (MAH-duhl)—a thing someone builds as an example of something larger to see how it will look or work

runway (RUHN-way)—a strip of hard, level ground that airplanes use for taking off and landing

sped (SPED)—moved at a fast rate

tease (TEEZ)—to say unkind things to someone in a way that is meant to be playful

turbulence (TUR-byuh-lens)—currents in the atmosphere that cause an airplane to move up and down

Discussion Questions

1. Katie flew on an airplane to visit her grandma. Have you flown on an airplane? Where did you go? If you haven't flown on an airplane, where do you want to fly someday?

2. Katie thinks her teddy bear is missing in the airport. Talk about a time when you thought something of yours was lost.

3. Katie was bored in the airport. She was also bored on the plane . . . until the turbulence started! What is something that you think is boring? Is there anything that can make it fun?

Writing Prompts

1. Write down three facts about airplanes. If you can't think of three, ask a grown-up to help you find some in a book or on the computer.

2. Imagine what it's like to fly a plane. What things do you see from the front of the plane? What do you do? Who helps you? Write a paragraph describing what you imagine.

3. Pretend you are Katie writing a letter to JoJo and Pedro on your plane ride. What do you tell them about your adventure?

Cooking with Katie Woo!

Up, up, and away! Make a friend a special treat with this fun project. These cool airplanes are made out of different types of candy. Ask a grown-up if you need help, and don't forget to wash your hands.

Candy Airplanes

What you need:

- two Life Saver candies
- a thin rubber band
- a roll of Smarties candy or other candies with a similar shape
- a stick of gum, with the foil and paper wrap on it
- optional: stickers, markers, crayons, etc.

What you do:

1. Thread the rubber band through the two Life Saver candies.

2. Balance the roll of Smarties between the Life Savers, across the rubber band.

3. Balance the gum on top of the Smarties and pull the rubber band up and over each side of the gum so that it is held in place. The gum will make your wings.

4. If you wish, decorate the wings with drawings, stickers, etc.

Your friends will love these airplanes. Give them as valentines, as part of a birthday gift, or just because!

THE FUN DOESN'T STOP HERE!

Discover more at www.capstonekids.com

- Videos & Contests
- Games & Puzzles
- Friends & Favorites
- Authors & Illustrators

Find cool websites and more books like this one at www.facthound.com. Just type in the Book ID: **9781479521753** and you're ready to go!